HOW TO
SCARE A MONSTER

Published by Muslim Children's Books

muslimchildrensbooks.co.uk

Published by Muslim Children's Books 2018
© Zanib Mian, 2018

Moral rights asserted.

ISBN 978-0-9955406-6-8

HOW TO
SCARE A MONSTER
ZANIB MIAN

Muslim Children's Books

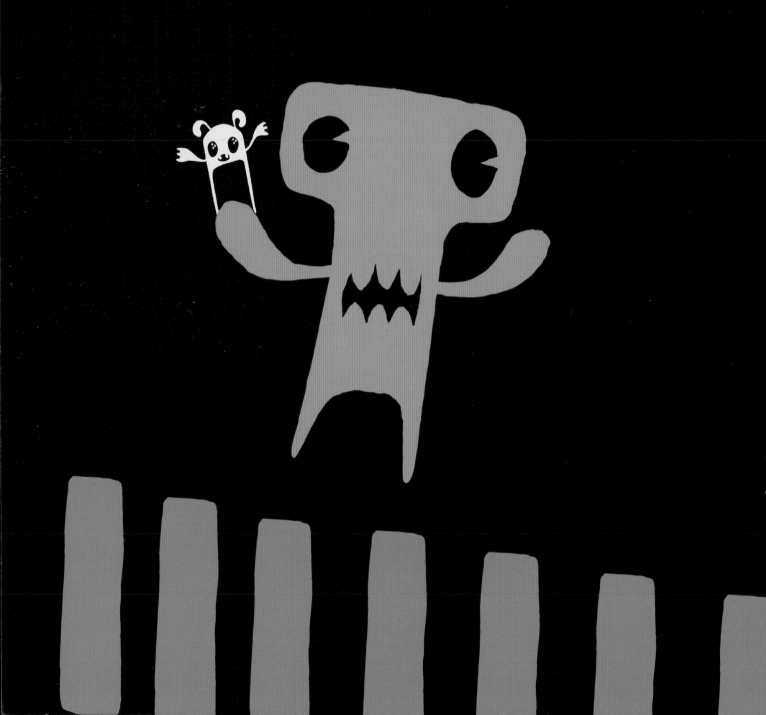

IF THERE'S A

MONSTER

AROUND,

YOU COULD

TRY

TO BE

FRIENDS

WITH IT.

OR...

YOU COULD CLOSE YOUR EYES AND PRETEND IT'S NOT THERE,

OR...

BUT THE ONLY WAY
TO GET RID OF
A MONSTER,

IS TO

SCARE IT.

MOST PEOPLE

TRY TO

R RROOAAAARR !

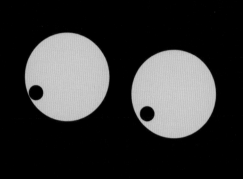

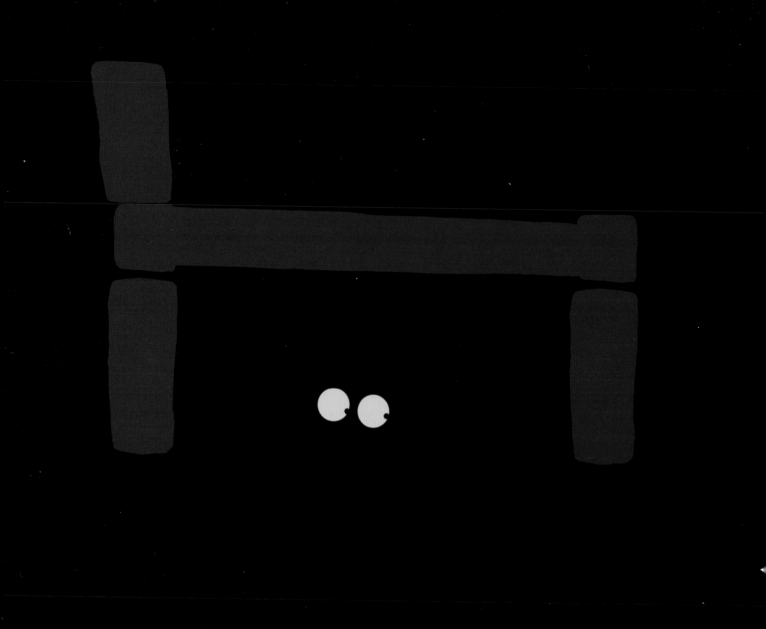

OR HIDE

UNDER THE

BED.

SOMETIMES, THEY CALL THEIR MUM,

OR EVEN BETTER,
A KID WITH A STINK-BOMB
IN THEIR NAPPY.

SOME TURN THE LIGHTS ON,

OR HOLD ON TO THEIR FAVOURITE TEDDY,

BUT NONE OF THAT WORKS,

NOT REALLY...

THE ONLY WAY

TO SCARE A MONSTER...

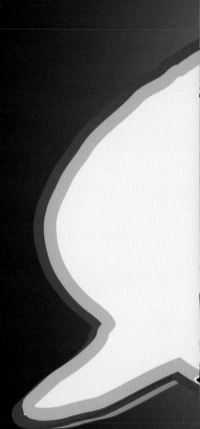

AuDHooBILLAH

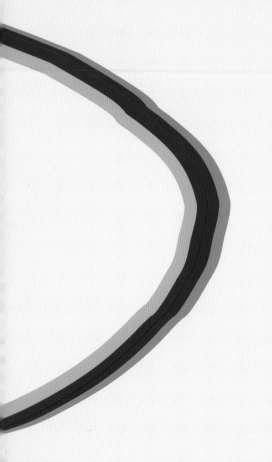

MONSTERS
RUN AWAY WHEN THEY HEAR THAT. REALLY *FAST*.

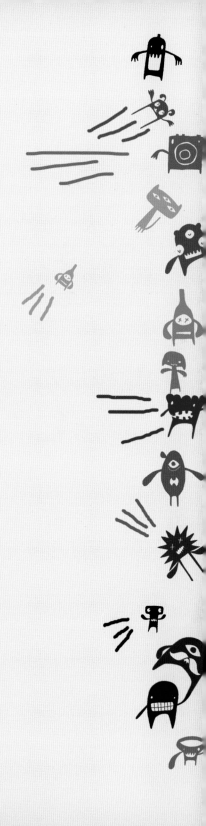

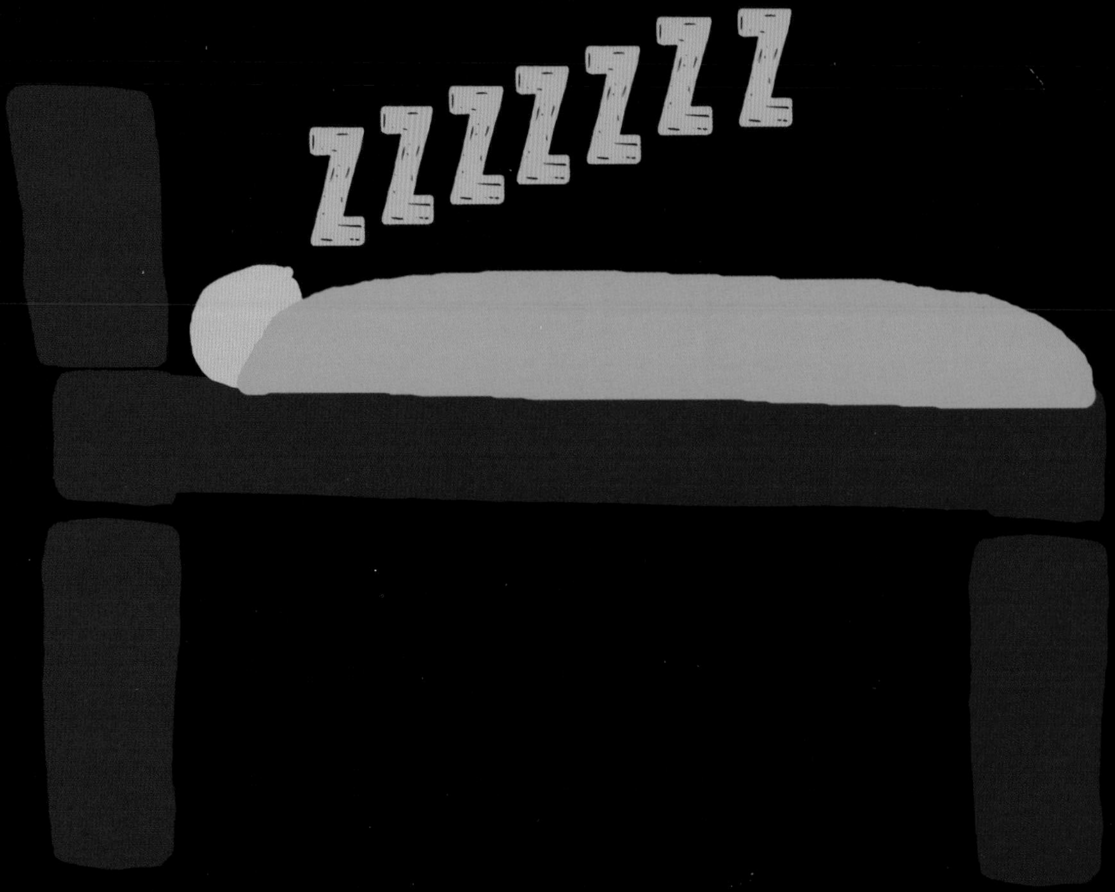
ZZZZZZZ

EVERY
TIME.

Other fantastic titles by Zanib Mian at muslimchildrensbooks.co.uk

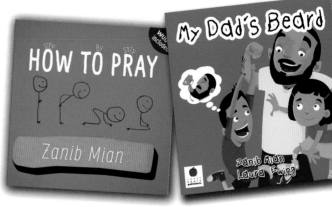

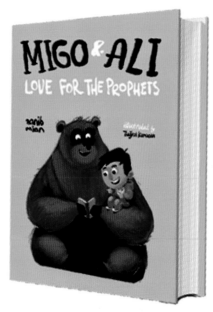

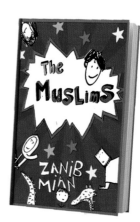